The Forest Fairy Pony

For the magical Gwion & Arwen
—SARAH KILBRIDE

To Paul
—SOPHIE TILLEY

ALADDIN
An imprint of Simon & Schuster Children's Publishing Division
1230 Avenue of the Americas, New York, New York 10020
First Aladdin paperback edition June 2021
Text copyright © 2014 by Sarah KilBride
Cover illustration copyright © 2021 by Paula Franco
Interior illustrations based on artwork originated by Sophie Tilley copyright © 2014
Originally published in Great Britain in 2014 by Simon & Schuster UK Ltd.
Also available in an Aladdin hardcover edition.
All rights reserved, including the right of reproduction in whole or in part in any form.
ALADDIN and related logo are registered trademarks of Simon & Schuster, Inc.
For information about special discounts for bulk purchases, please contact Simon & Schuster Special Sales at 1-866-506-1949 or business@simonandschuster.com.
The Simon & Schuster Speakers Bureau can bring authors to your live event. For more information or to book an event contact the Simon & Schuster Speakers Bureau at 1-866-248-3049 or visit our website at www.simonspeakers.com.
Cover designed by Tiara Iandiorio
The text of this book was set in Sabon LT Std.
Manufactured in the United States of America 0421 OFF
2 4 6 8 10 9 7 5 3 1
Library of Congress Cataloging-in-Publication Data
Names: KilBride, Sarah, author. | Tilley, Sophie, illustrator.
Title: Forest fairy pony / by Sarah KilBride ; interior illustrations by Sophie Tilley.
Description: First Aladdin paperback edition. | New York : Aladdin, 2021. |
Series: [Princess Evie ; 1] | Audience: Ages 6 to 9. | Summary: Princess Evie feels anxious about starting a new school, but she gains confidence after she visits an enchanted forest with her magical pony and helps a forest fairy named Holly welcome new forest fairy pupils on their first day of fairy school.
Identifiers: LCCN 2020051869 (print) | LCCN 2020051870 (ebook) |
ISBN 9781534476288 (hardcover) | ISBN 9781534476271 (paperback) |
ISBN 9781534476295 (ebook)
Subjects: CYAC: Princessess—Fiction. | Fairies—Fiction. | Schools—Fiction. | Ponies—Fiction.
Classification: LCC PZ7.K55444 Fo 2021 (print) | LCC PZ7.K55444 (ebook) |
DDC [Fic]—dc23
LC record available at https://lccn.loc.gov/2020051869
LC ebook record available at https://lccn.loc.gov/2020051870

Princess EVIE

By Sarah KilBride

Interior illustrations by
Sophie Tilley

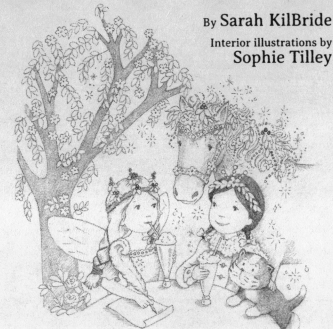

The Forest Fairy Pony

ALADDIN
NEW YORK   LONDON   TORONTO   SYDNEY   NEW DELHI

CHAPTER 1

Sleepyhead

Princess Evie woke with a start. *Wow, everyone must still be asleep*, thought Evie. Even Sparkles! Her kitten was usually at the door first thing in the morning waking Evie up with a noisy meow, but Starlight Castle was completely silent. Evie snuggled up under her cozy feather duvet and sighed. *I'll have to wake up earlier than this on Monday*, she thought to herself. *I'll need plenty of time to feed my ponies before getting ready for the first day at my new school!*

Evie loved her beautiful ponies. They weren't like any other ponies—each one of them was magic. There was a tunnel of trees at Starlight Stables that no one else knew about, and whenever Evie rode one of her ponies through the tunnel of trees they were whisked away on a magical adventure in a faraway land. As they galloped out of the tunnel, Evie's ponies would be magically transformed, their manes and tails glittering and their coats swirling with different colors, and Evie would be wearing an exquisite new outfit.

Evie sat up in her four-poster bed and rubbed her sleepy eyes. She smiled as she remembered all the places that her ponies had taken her and the

wonderful friends she'd met—forest
fairies, cloud sprites, and even polar
bears! Souvenirs from her adventures
were dotted around her room: a wand
from Foxwood School of Magic, a
silver bracelet with the precious pink
pearl from Periwinkle the mermaid,
and, on the marble mantelpiece, the

snowflake necklace given to her by the ice pixies. Even her purple silk pajamas were a souvenir from a magical desert sleepover with the seven star princesses!

"How am I ever going to find time to have adventures with my ponies when I'm at school?" Evie wondered out loud as she jumped down from her bed. She landed softly on her white fluffy rug and shivered. The fire had gone out in the grate and her big bedroom felt chilly. Evie quickly slipped on her coral-pink dressing gown and slippers and padded over to the window to open the thick velvet curtains. The sun was beginning to shine, making Starlight Stables sparkle.

I've got to make the most of my

*magic ponies before school starts
tomorrow,* Evie decided. *I'm so lucky
to have them.* While Evie was thinking
about her ponies, she heard a loud
meow at her bedroom door.

"How are you this morning,
Sparkles?" asked Evie, opening the
door.

Sparkles trotted in, his eyes twinkling. He looked wide-awake and ready to go!

"Meow!" said Sparkles as he began to clean his paws.

"You're right, Sparkles! It's time to get washed and dressed. We've got a busy morning ahead of us and we haven't got a second to lose. Now then," said Evie as she went to her wardrobe, "where's my pink dress and stripy tights?"

Evie pushed her wardrobe doors open to find the outfit she always wore when she went to the stables. Her wardrobe was bursting with gorgeous pink, purple, and silver clothes.

She looked at her flower dresses sewn with silk, her rainbow socks, and her fluffy boots.

"I'm going to miss wearing all these clothes," said Evie sadly. "From tomorrow on I'll have to wear a uniform."

Sparkles jumped up onto the windowsill and stepped carefully around the framed photos of Evie's ponies. He looked at Evie's uniform

and then back at Evie and blinked
slowly. Even though he was only a
cat, Evie was sure he understood
everything.

"You're right, Sparkles, my new
uniform is very stylish."

It was hanging on the wardrobe's
mirrored doors, ready for tomorrow.

"And of course, I'll still be able
to wear all my other clothes on the
weekends." This thought cheered Evie
up and soon she was washed, dressed,
and ready for breakfast.

Evie met Sparkles at the top of the
huge staircase that spiraled down
to the hall. It was lined with golden
framed portraits of Evie's ancestors.
Some of them were on horseback,
and Evie always wondered whether

they rode through the tunnel of trees like she did—the castle was full of ornaments and trinkets from faraway places.

"On your mark, get set, go!"

They raced past the paintings, through the echoing hall, and down into the kitchen.

"Sparkles—you won again!" laughed Evie. "You always do!"

The table was set with ruby raspberries, silver-birch syrup, and delicious homemade jams. Evie tucked into her breakfast, and by the time she was spreading her favorite jam onto her crumpets, Sparkles's bowl was empty and the little kitten was busy licking his paws. Sparkles loved the weekends because he always had kippers for breakfast. What a treat!

"I wish you could come to school with me. I won't know anyone." Evie tried to imagine her new classroom and teacher. She felt a little shiver and couldn't decide whether she was feeling nervous or excited.

CHAPTER 2

Pony Preparations

"Come on," said Evie as she put on her rain boots, "let's go and feed the ponies." Evie loved this part of the day—her ponies were always so glad to see her. They whinnied and neighed as soon as they heard Evie and her kitten making their way through the castle grounds. "Let's take the shortcut through the orchard," said Evie, "and we can collect some windfall apples for a tasty pony treat!"

Evie could see Silver waiting for her

at the gate with her friends Shimmer
and Indigo. Silver was a pretty Welsh
mountain pony and Evie's smallest, but
without a doubt she was the strongest
pony Evie had ever met! Star, Evie's
spirited Arab, neighed from her stable.
Star loved nothing more than racing
along the mountaintops with the

wind in her mane. All her ponies were
extremely special and Evie loved each
one of them.

There was always so much to do at
Starlight Stables, but the first job was
to make sure her ponies were all happy
and to give them fresh water. The sun
was beginning to warm the autumn

air, and little leaves fluttered from the trees. As Evie led her ponies from the field and tied them in the stable yard, Sparkles played with the leaves, jumping and pouncing and trying to bat them with his paws.

It wasn't long before Evie called over to her kitten, "Time to get to work, Sparkles."

It wasn't just Evie's ponies that enjoyed eating oats! Sparkles had the very important job of making sure Starlight Stables was free of rats and mice. Evie opened the door and Sparkles dashed in to inspect the feed shed.

After a few minutes, he gave a loud "all clear" meow!

"Phew!" said Evie.

Evie went in and measured out the
oats. Each one of her ponies had a
different amount because they were
all different shapes and sizes. Some of
Evie's ponies were energetic, like her
Arab, Star, while others liked to take

things a little easier! Added to that, some of them spent their time out in the fields, enjoying the grass, while others lived in their stables.

While the ponies were enjoying their breakfasts, Evie got her grooming kit from the tack room and brushed their coats and cleaned out their feet. She checked that her ponies didn't have any injuries and chatted away to them.

"If anyone heard me talking to you like this, Willow," said Evie as she looked over her little New Forest pony's feet, "they might think I was crazy!" But Evie knew talking to her ponies made them feel calm.

Willow stood at thirteen hands. Like all New Forests, she was gentle and very sure-footed. As Evie combed out her thick mane, Willow nudged her gently.

"You're right, Willow," said Evie. "It is the perfect day for an adventure."

Evie went to the tack room to get

her pony's saddle and bridle. The walls were lined with saddle racks and hooks for every bridle and halter.

Hanging next to Willow's saddle were all her rosettes. Although Willow wasn't the fastest pony at Starlight Stables, she was a great jumper and she loved going to cross-country events with Evie.

It didn't take long to saddle Willow up.

Evie was about to mount when she remembered something very important!

"Of course we can't go yet! We have to take my backpack of useful things!" Evie could never go through the tunnel of trees without her backpack—there was always something in it that they needed.

When Sparkles saw Evie putting
the backpack on, he raced across the
yard and sprang up into the saddle. He
adored going on adventures with Evie

and her magic ponies; they always had so much fun.

Soon Willow was trotting out of Starlight Stables, taking Evie and Sparkles toward the tunnel of trees. Evie closed her eyes and took a deep breath.

Where would it take them today?

CHAPTER 3

Old Forest Friends

"What a beautiful forest," gasped Evie
as they came into a clearing of tall trees.

Willow's coat swirled with autumn
colors and her mane was decorated
with shining berries. Sparkling
dewdrops glimmered like diamonds
along her browband.

A gentle breeze blew through the
trees, but Evie was nice and warm.
She was wearing a scarf as delicate as
a cobweb and a pale green felt jacket
that tied at the waist with a ribbon the

color of blackberries. Her skirt was
layered with different shades of pink
silk like the petals of a wild rose.

Willow neighed as they came to a halt.

"You're right, Willow, we have
been here before—for the forest fairy

fashion show. We helped the forest fairies to make their outfits with spiders' webs and dewdrops."

"And you helped us to solve the mystery of the stolen dresses," said a voice from above. "Welcome back."

Evie looked up.

"Holly!" laughed Evie. "How lovely to see you again!"

The forest fairy fluttered down from her branch and gave Evie a hug. She was a little bit older and taller than Evie, and her blue eyes sparkled with happiness to see her friend again.

"I'm so glad you've come back," said the forest fairy, stroking Willow's muzzle. "We've got a busy day ahead of us. Let's go to the Acorn Café and I'll tell you all about it."

Holly led the way, flying in and out of the trees. Evie felt the warm autumn sun on her face and the fresh crisp air. It wasn't long before Evie and Holly were busily catching up on each other's news.

"I've been chosen to teach all the new fairies how to become magic forest fairies," said Holly. "They'll be arriving in a little while. As it's their first day at forest fairy school, I'll help them settle in with a fun task before teaching them all about forest magic."

"I'm starting a new school too," said Evie. "I'm feeling a bit nervous about it."

"When do you start?" asked Holly.

"Tomorrow," said Evie. "I hope my

new teacher will be as kind as you, Holly, and gives us time to settle in." Holly fluttered down and held Evie's hand.

"I feel so unsure about everything. There are so many things I want to know," said Evie, trying to smile. "What will the other girls be like? What happens at break times? The more I think about it, the more fluttery I feel!"

Holly smiled at her friend. "What you're feeling is completely natural. All the new fairies will be feeling nervous today, but it won't take long for the fun to start and the friendships to begin. Just you see."

In no time at all, they arrived at the Acorn Café.

"Here we are, Willow," said Evie,
giving her pony one of the windfall
apples from Starlight Castle's orchard
and some fresh water.

"Mmmm, let's order some hazelnut

shakes," said Holly, looking at the
menu. "They're yummy!"

They sat down at a table with their
delicious shakes. Holly made a list
of things to do with her magic quill,
which was made from a magnificent
golden feather.

"We have got a busy morning ahead

27

of us!" said Evie, looking at the long list. "We'd better get started."

"Let's split up," said Holly, finishing her shake. "That way we'll get everything done quickly. Willow can take you into the forest to collect birch bark and firewood for the campfire. See you back in the Magic Dell!"

CHAPTER 4

A Wonderful Welcome

Evie and Sparkles hopped onto Willow and disappeared into the forest while Holly made a list of all the new fairies' names. As she called out each name, her magic quill wrote them down:

"Ivy, Arwen, Rose, Sylvette, Rowan, Bryony, Juniper, Violet, Faye . . ."

When she'd finished, Holly made a map for each fairy. As she described the woods, her magic quill drew a map of Bluebell Forest. Evie didn't need one to find the silver birch trees because her New Forest pony knew exactly where to go.

"This papery birch bark is perfect for starting campfires," said Evie as she carefully peeled the birch tree's trunk. Then Sparkles and Willow helped her find dry sticks for kindling.

Evie met Holly back at the Magic Dell and they built the campfire.

"We'll light it at the end of the day," said Holly as they arranged cushions on the forest floor.

"We've only got ten minutes before the new fairies arrive!" said Evie. "And we've still got lots to do!"

"I'll make the signposts and find a wand for each fairy," said Holly, looking at the list. "Could you decorate

these baskets please, Evie? They need
to be sorted into pairs and for each
pair to look identical."

Evie looked at the little baskets.

"Shall I paint each pair the same
color?" she asked.

"That's a great idea, but we haven't got time for the paint to dry," said Holly. "I'm sure you'll think of something, though!"

Holly set to work drawing beautiful signs with her magic quill and then whizzed off into the forest to put the signs up, while Evie sorted the baskets into pairs.

"How am I ever going to make these pairs look identical, Sparkles?" asked Evie, picking up two of the baskets. Her kitten began diving about in the fallen leaves.

"What a brilliant idea, Sparkles! Of course—I'll decorate each pair with a different type of leaf!"

Evie set to work. She decorated two of the baskets with oak leaves and

acorns, and another two with orange
beech leaves and beech nuts. Sparkles
helped her collect a pile of pretty
rowan leaves and red berries for the
next two. Very soon all the baskets
were matching pairs.

When Holly returned, she was
delighted. "They look lovely," she smiled.

But Evie was looking a little confused.

"There are nine names on the register," she said. "But we've got ten baskets."

"One of them is yours," smiled Holly, popping a wand into each basket. "I hope you don't mind, but I had an odd number of fairies in my class, so I needed you to help make up a pair."

"No problem," said Evie, who was happy to help her friend.

Now they were ready for the new forest fairies!

One after another, the new fairies began to arrive at the Magic Dell. Some of them looked a little bit lost. Some of them looked a little bit sad. Some fluttered at the edges of the circle and

a few laughed a little too loud. Evie
realized that they were all feeling
nervous and that each of them showed
their nerves in a different way.

Holly, Evie, and Sparkles tried to
make the fairies feel better with a
friendly smile. They asked each fairy
their name and gave them each a
basket. Everyone sat down on the comfy
cushions and the nervous chattering
stopped. The forest fell silent.

"Welcome to Bluebell Forest," smiled
Holly. "Today is all about learning how
to fly and find your way in this magic
forest. Take your time and use all your
senses to navigate.

"In a few minutes you will be
exploring the forest and making your

very own fairy crowns. You will have a partner to help you and I'll never be far away."

Evie looked around the circle as Holly talked and wondered which fairy was going to be her partner.

"Your partner is the fairy with the same basket as you."

Evie's basket was decorated with ivy leaves.

She looked around and soon spotted the other fairy with an ivy basket. The fairy had golden hair and a lovely smile. Evie walked over to her.

"Hello," she said. "I'm Evie."

"I'm Arwen," smiled her partner. "Is that your magic forest pony?"

"Yes, that's Willow," said Evie. "She'd love to take us into the forest. Come on!"

Evie and Sparkles hopped up onto Willow's back, while Arwen hovered above them.

"You will discover that the forest

is full of life; it's home to many creatures. Work with them and they will help your magic," said Holly. "Everyone needs to be back here with their finished crowns by the time the blackbirds begin to sing."

The fairies started looking at their maps and getting ready to leave. Soon they were all fluttering into Bluebell Forest with their partners.

CHAPTER 5

New Friends

"I've never flown in the forest before," said Arwen nervously as she took off. "I'm not sure if I'm good enough to do it."

"Don't worry," said Evie, "we'll take it slow. I think it's a bit like riding a pony through the forest—keep your balance and don't rush. Once you get the hang of it, you'll love it—we do, don't we, Willow?"

Willow tossed her mane and flicked her lovely tail.

"The secret is to look where you're going but remember to keep your eyes open for any challenges up ahead. You don't want a nasty surprise like a branch in the face!"

Willow walked in and out of the trees. Arwen flew above the New Forest pony and began to feel more confident.

"You're looking great!" said Evie. "Are you ready to go a bit faster?"

"Absolutely!" The little fairy smiled.

Willow began to trot along the forest path.

"When you're coming to a corner, make sure you're not going too fast. You don't want to lose your balance!" said Evie. Arwen watched how Evie helped to steer Willow and slow her down if there was a tight corner coming up. Arwen copied this and soon she was weaving through the trees effortlessly.

"This is brilliant!" laughed Arwen

as they sailed over ditches. "You and
Willow are such a great team!"

Arwen was right—Willow loved
riding cross-country with Evie, and
Evie was a careful rider. She could feel
the fresh air whiz past them as they
raced through the forest. They were
having so much fun racing up slopes
and following streams that for a while
they forgot their task!

It was only when Willow came to a halt by a cluster of hazel trees draped with strings of little leaves and red berries that the friends remembered they had to make forest fairy crowns.

"Why don't we use these?" said Evie. "We can twist the stems to make a crown."

Arwen and Evie each took a string of leaves and twisted it into a circle.

"Let's try them on," said Arwen.

"They'll look really beautiful when we decorate them," said Evie, helping Arwen to tighten her crown a little.

"You're right, but what can we use?"

At that moment a beautiful gold feather floated down from the tree. Shimmering on a branch above was the most striking golden bird.

"Please, could we have a few more of
your feathers?" asked Evie hopefully,
carefully fixing the feather onto
Arwen's crown.

The bird looked down at them, her

bright eyes flickering like flames.

"I think she's a phoenix," whispered Evie. "I've read about them in one of the old books in Starlight Castle's library. I thought they were mythical creatures."

The golden bird screeched at them, making poor Willow jump and Sparkles shake. It was a shock that such a beautiful bird could make such a terrible sound!

"She sounds real to me!" said Arwen. The phoenix squawked again.

"I think she's trying to tell us something," said Evie, putting her hands over her ears. "Perhaps you could try some forest magic to translate."

"I've never tried any forest magic

before," said Arwen, carefully taking her wand out of her basket. "But I'll give it a try."

"Take your time," said Evie.

Arwen closed her eyes and after a few seconds began whispering some magic forest words:

"Blow, wind, blow,
Golden bird, do not shriek.
Flow, words, flow,
Golden words from your beak.
Leaves shiver, leaves fall,
Forest creature, tell me all."

Tiny green sparks fizzed and whizzed from the tip of the wand and floated above their heads.

The phoenix stood tall and opened her mouth, but instead of letting out another shrill shriek, she said in a proud voice:

"Look around the forest trees,
Listen to the forest breeze.
A little pincushion trying to sleep,
Help him—he's in trouble deep.
When you've finished this task at hand,
I will help you gild your band."

And with that, she flew a little
farther up into the tree.

"I hope you're better at solving
riddles than I am," said Evie.

"Hmm," said Arwen thoughtfully.
"I think the second part of the riddle

means the phoenix will help us with our crowns if we help someone in the forest. But I don't know who they are or where we'll find them."

Arwen and Evie looked at the map of Bluebell Forest, searching for clues.

"A pincushion would be used by someone sewing," said Evie. "Perhaps they're making outfits with spiderweb thread like we did for the fashion show."

"But where would they be?" asked Arwen. Willow neighed loudly.

"I think Willow knows," said Evie.

CHAPTER 6

Pincushion in a Pickle

In just a few moments, Evie and Sparkles were cantering through the forest on Willow's back, with Arwen flying above. As they went deeper into the forest, Willow had to jump branches and trees that had fallen across the path.

"I love the way you help Willow jump, Evie," Arwen called down. Evie leaned forward as Willow took off over a branch.

"If there's something in the way, you have to make sure you're going at it straight and steady. It's the same for you, Arwen, when you're flying over obstacles."

"I think Willow trusts you because you never push her too hard."

"I trust her too," smiled Evie. "We look out for each other."

It was true Willow trusted Evie; the brave little pony didn't mind if she couldn't see where she was going to land after taking off over a fallen branch because she knew Evie would never ask too much of her.

Arwen flew above them, the wind whistling through her hair.

"Hold on to your crown, Evie," she called down to her friend as they raced through the trees.

After a short while, they came to a

clearing with a tall sycamore tree. Evie
stroked Willow's neck.

"Good girl," she smiled as she
and Sparkles hopped down from the
saddle.

"Now all we need to find is a pincushion," said Arwen, landing gently and looking through the piles of autumn leaves.

But the friends couldn't find anything like a pincushion.

"Maybe we're not in the right place after all," said Evie.

They began to walk through the shady forest, searching the mossy floor, when Sparkles's whiskers began to twitch.

"Whatever's the matter, Sparkles?" said Evie.

Willow stopped and the little kitten jumped about and started searching around in the roots of a tree.

Evie spotted a shiny nose and a pair of bright eyes peeping at them from

the shadows—and out popped a baby
hedgehog!

"A little pincushion!" she cried.
"Sparkles, you've solved the riddle!"

The little hedgehog came out of
his hiding place and began making
excitable squeaky noises.

"How are we going to help this little hedgehog out?" said Arwen.

"What on earth is he trying to tell us?" asked Evie.

Arwen whisked out her wand and performed the translation spell:

"Blow, wind, blow,
Prickly hedgehog, do not squeak.
Flow, words, flow,
Little hedge pig, try to speak.
Leaves shiver, leaves fall,
Forest creature, tell me all."

Tiny green sparks fizzed and whizzed again from the tip of her wand and floated above them.

"Follow me. Come along—I want to show you something. I've been working hard all day. Come and have a little look; come and see what I've built. It's

beautiful, my new house. I've tried to
wake up my friends to show them, but
they're all asleep. They usually wake
up around now to look for some nice
berries to eat. Come on, keep up . . ."
The little hedgehog's words tumbled out.

"What a chatterbox!" giggled Evie.

They had quite a job keeping up with the little creature, who was chittering away as he led them along the forest path. He was surprisingly fast and it seemed that he was in quite a hurry.

"I never knew hedgehogs could move so quickly," said Arwen.

He brought them to a pile of very untidy sticks and leaves.

"Here it is!" he said proudly. "My new home."

Arwen and Evie looked at each other, not sure what to say.

Evie peeped inside and could see a muddy puddle.

"It's not very cozy," she said.

"It's my first hibernation and I've worked very hard collecting all these

leaves and sticks. It's taken me a long,
long, long time to build this."

Evie didn't want to hurt the little
hedgehog's feelings.

"How very clever of you to disguise
your house to look like a pile of old

leaves," she smiled. "But when the winter comes and it gets colder, I'm sure you'd like it to be nice and dry inside."

"Perhaps we could build your nest somewhere else, somewhere drier," said Arwen. "I think Sparkles may have found just the spot!"

Sparkles was sitting in a sheltered patch beneath a little bush, next to some brambles.

"Perfect," said the hedgehog. "I love blackberries!"

"You won't have to go far for lunch!" agreed Arwen.

The friends set to work, helping the little hedgehog to build his winter nest.

"We'll need lots of dry leaves, little sticks, grass, and some moss," said Evie.

"These might do," said Arwen with
an armful of leaves.

Suddenly the girls heard the sound of
a rotten branch snapping. They froze.
It felt like someone was watching
them—but who could it be?

Arwen took hold of her wand and
searched the undergrowth. The air

began to shimmer and, after a moment, Holly appeared!

"I didn't know you could make yourself invisible!" laughed Evie, relieved to see it was her friend.

"I've come to see how you're doing," said Holly.

"We've started our crowns," said Arwen. Evie and Arwen showed Holly their handiwork. "But we need to help this little pincushion before we can finish them."

"I'm so pleased you're helping a forest creature," said Holly. "Keep up the good work! I can't wait to see your beautiful crowns when they're finished." And with that, Holly gave them both a quick hug and was gone!

Arwen and Evie helped the hedgehog make a pile with the leaves, moss, and

grass they had collected. The little
hedgehog then climbed to the top of the
mound and burrowed inside, turning
around and around, packing the leaves
flat.

Together, they had made a beautiful
cozy nest with thick walls.

"Let's celebrate with a feast!" said the delighted hedgehog, and they all helped themselves to the delicious blackberries growing on the bramble next door.

The berries were very juicy and soon Evie, Arwen, and the little hedgehog

were covered in the berries' purple juices.

"I'll see if I've got anything to wipe our fingers with," said Evie as she opened up her backpack of useful things. She pulled out a pink silk handkerchief and, as she did so, a single woolen mitten fell out too.

"I don't think that'll be any good at cleaning us up," laughed Arwen, "but it might help a little hedgehog keep snug in the winter."

Arwen was right! It made a perfect bed for the hedgehog. Evie carefully laid it in his nest.

"Do you know the quickest way back to the phoenix?" asked Evie. But the little hedgehog didn't hear her, as he was already scurrying away to wake

up his friends and invite them to his
nest-warming party!

"We'll find our way back," said
Arwen. "I feel like I'm getting to know
the forest."

"It won't take us long," said Evie.
"Especially with Willow to carry us!"

CHAPTER 7

A Nasty Surprise

They set off along the forest path.
It was just as well that Willow was
sure-footed because the ground soon
changed from being soft and squidgy
to stony and slippery. One minute
Willow was trotting through piles of
crisp leaves that reached her feathery
fetlocks and the next she was picking
her way through sticky mud.

Arwen was relieved she could fly
over this rough terrain, and Sparkles
was very glad that he didn't have to
walk through it, especially the mud!

When they came to some fallen branches, Willow refused to jump even a small one. Evie knew something was not right.

"What's wrong, Willow?" whispered Evie as she turned Willow to take the jump again, and then Evie realized.

"You're limping," she cried. Evie dismounted right away. When she looked into Willow's eyes, she could see her pony was in pain.

"What if it's something serious?" Evie's heart was pounding, but she had to control her feeling of panic.

"It's her front right leg," said Arwen. The little fairy held Willow's reins and talked quietly to her to reassure her and keep her calm.

"I can't see any cuts or scratches," said Evie, peering closely at her pony's leg.

Gently, she ran her hand over
Willow's shoulder and leg to check for
swelling or heat. Willow didn't flinch.
Next Evie carefully picked up her
pony's hoof.

"No wonder you're limping,
Willow," gasped Evie. "You've got a
sharp stone lodged in your hoof."

It was near the heart-shaped pad at the center of the hoof, called the frog. Luckily, Evie kept her hoof pick in her backpack, but she knew she would have to be extra careful as Willow's hoof would be more sensitive than usual.

"You're going to have to be a very brave pony," she said as she cautiously removed the forest debris around the stone. "Let's hope it hasn't damaged your hoof."

They were lucky—the stone fell out from Willow's hoof and Evie saw that, although her sole wasn't punctured, there was a nasty purple bruise. Evie knew that this would be very painful for quite some time.

"The best treatment is to rest for a few days," said Evie.

"But you can't stay here in the

middle of the forest," said Arwen.

A golden feather floated down. There above the girls was the shimmering phoenix.

"Can you help us, phoenix?" asked Evie.

The golden bird flew down and landed on Arwen's shoulder.

"Together we can heal Willow," the phoenix said. "Follow me, Arwen."

And with that, they disappeared into the forest. Evie turned to her pony and blinked back tears.

She knew she had to be brave for Willow's sake, but she could see her pony was in a lot of pain and Evie began to wonder if it was her fault. As Evie stroked Willow, she could feel her pony relax and lean in to her.

"We'll look after you," she whispered in her ear. "Just you see."

After a few minutes Arwen returned
with a handful of magic herbs. The
phoenix wasn't far behind Arwen, with
some moss in her beak.

"These will heal Willow's hoof," said
Arwen.

She mixed the herbs, moss, and
some clay from the ground and made a
poultice. She placed the dressing gently
onto Willow's bruise. Then the phoenix
rested her magical golden wings on the

injured hoof and, as she did this, Arwen lifted her wand and tiny green sparks floated from the tip. Willow closed her eyes as the magic began to glow, and Arwen and the phoenix worked together to heal Willow's hoof.

"I think that's done the trick," said Arwen as she gently took the poultice away. "Yes, your bruise has vanished."

"Thank you," smiled Evie. Tears welled up in her eyes again, but this time they were tears of happiness! She was so relieved to see that her pony's injury was healed. Willow tossed her long mane and stamped her foot as if she were raring to go!

"Before you leave," said the phoenix, "look closely at this tree."

"It's hollow!" said Evie.

"It's a fairy tree," explained the golden bird.

Arwen took a peek inside the hollow trunk.

"It's full of treasure!" she gasped.

Inside was a pile of little sycamore leaves made from real gold, and glittering among them were jewels that looked just like shining blackberries.

"Our crowns will be magnificent,"
said Evie. "Thank you, phoenix."

The phoenix bowed her head
majestically, and with that, she
disappeared into the golden canopy of
the forest.

"Let me help you, Evie," said Arwen.

The girls threaded the precious
leaves and berries into their forest
crowns and even laced a few into
Willow's mane. When they had
finished, there were still some golden
leaves and jewels left.

"Let's take these back for the
others," Evie suggested.

"Good idea, Evie!"

Willow's hoof was so much better
that she was able to trot along the
forest path, taking Evie and Sparkles
back to the dell. Arwen fluttered along

after them, carefully carrying her
basket of treasure.

As they got closer to the Magic Dell,
they could see wisps of smoke and
the air was full of blackbirds' song
and fairies' laughter. It sounded like
everyone had enjoyed their first day.

CHAPTER 8

Campfire Catch-Up

"Welcome back!" smiled Holly. "I hope you've had fun in the forest—I can't wait to hear about it!"

Soon all the fairies had returned safely back to the dell and were sitting around the campfire, warm and happy.

"I'm so glad you enjoyed your forest adventures," said Holly. "Now, who wants to go first and tell everyone about their day?"

Faye put up her hand and she and her partner began to tell everyone how they had helped a little squirrel hide all the hazelnuts he'd collected for his winter store. As they told their story, they handed out some of the deliciously crunchy nuts.

Next the fairies listened to how Bryony and Violet had made warm winter coats for a family of dormice. They had used fur from the insides of chestnut shells and had brought a basketful of the creamy chestnuts to roast in the glowing fire.

Then it was Evie and Arwen's turn to tell their story of how they had helped the little hedgehog build his nest. Everyone was looking forward to the blackberries Arwen and Evie had picked with the hedgehog, and a few fairies looked a bit disappointed when Evie told them they had eaten them all.

"We've got something else to share
with you," said Arwen.

Evie and Arwen handed out the
gold leaves and bright jewels that

they had found in the fairy tree. The
fairies gasped and wove them into
their crowns, where they sparkled
and glittered in the firelight. As the

fairies took turns telling their stories,
it became obvious that they had all
helped forest creatures in some way,
and in return the magnificent golden
phoenix had helped each of them.

Everyone had enjoyed their first day,
even though they had all felt nervous
about it at the start. It was clear that

friendships had already begun to blossom and everyone was looking forward to their second day in the forest.

"We worry about meeting new people and going to new places," said Holly. "It's impossible to imagine what it's going to be like, and that can make us feel anxious, but new people and new places can be fun too. First days are the start of an adventure!"

Soon the campfire was smoldering and it was time to go home. The fairies said goodbye to Sparkles, Willow, and Evie and wished Evie luck for her first day.

"Try not to worry about tomorrow," smiled little Faye.

"Everyone will be feeling the same as you," said Sylvette.

Bryony gave Evie a hug. "Stay calm and smile."

"And remember that the people

around you won't be strangers for long—soon they will be your friends," said Ivy and Violet, holding hands.

"Soon you'll know everyone's names and share many lovely times with your newfound friends," smiled Rowan and Rose, looking tired but happy. All the fairies fluttered up into the air and followed Juniper through the trees.

"Thank you for helping make my first day such an adventure," said Arwen, giving her new friend a hug.

"Thank you for looking after Willow," said Evie. "We've certainly had an unforgettable time!"

"Good luck tomorrow, and remember, it's the beginning of a great adventure," said Arwen.

"Thank you for all your help today, Evie. I hope you enjoy your first day

at school," said Holly, and then she
whispered a forest fairy secret into
Evie's ear.

Willow neighed as she took Evie and
Sparkles along the forest path back to
the tunnel of trees.

CHAPTER 9

Forest Fairy Secrets

Evie got back to Starlight Stables and untacked Willow and groomed her coat. When she cleaned out her hooves, it was hard to believe that Willow had been injured that day—there wasn't a mark to be seen.

"Thank you for taking me back to the forest, Willow. I've had a magical day. It was great to catch up with my old friend Holly and to make some lovely new friends too!"

Evie knew she should have an early night, but before she and Sparkles

could go back to the castle for some
supper and to get some sleep, she had
to clean her ponies' stables and make
sure they were ready for the night. Evie
checked their water and gave them all

fresh hay. She fed Willow some tasty carrots from the vegetable garden.

"I think you deserve a treat for working so hard and for being so brave today," she smiled, giving her pony a gentle hug.

When Evie was in her room, she emptied her backpack out onto her desk. She was looking for some nice pens and pencils to put in her new pencil case for tomorrow, when out fell a magnificent golden feather. She looked at the feather closely and realized what it was.

"It's a magic quill like Holly's," Evie gasped. "What a fantastic present. I'm sure it'll come in handy, especially when I have to do my homework. Thank you, forest fairies."

Sparkles watched Evie pack her

schoolbag and check her uniform.

"Do you know, Sparkles, I think I'm looking forward to tomorrow! I can't wait to make some new friends!"

Sparkles began purring loudly, then curled himself up into a little ball on Evie's comfy bed. He was exhausted!

"I'd better have an early night as well! There's nothing worse than being too tired to enjoy an adventure."

That night, Evie lay in her soft

feather bed and listened to the storm
that was blowing around Starlight
Castle's towers. She thought about her
ponies, safe in their stables, and the
animals they'd met in the forest—the
little hedgehog snug in his nest and
the proud phoenix in his golden tree.
Evie smiled and huddled up under her
toasty duvet; she knew she was going
to sleep well.

The next morning Evie woke to the

sound of her alarm clock. She'd set it extra early so she would have time to get ready for her first day without having to race around.

She hopped down from her bed and opened the curtains. The sky was clear and the sun was beginning to rise.

"Good morning, Starlight Stables," she smiled. "Today I'm going to have another adventure—my first day at my new school!"

When Evie had finished putting on her uniform, she turned to Sparkles, who was sitting on the windowsill.

"What do you think, Sparkles?"

Her little kitten looked carefully at Evie's pretty school shoes with their silver buckles and began to purr. After breakfast the two of them trotted down to the stables. Evie fed her ponies their breakfast.

"I'll tell you all about my first day when I get back," she whispered to Willow. Willow whinnied as if to wish Evie luck.

It was time to go. As Evie shut the gate, she felt a little flutter of nervousness, or was it excitement? The wind blew and leaves flew around her. Evie remembered Holly's forest fairy secret and she held out her hand and caught a golden leaf.

With the leaf held in both hands, Evie closed her eyes, just as Holly had told her to do, then blew the leaf back into the wind, and made her wish:

"I wish that . . .

. . . everyone has a magical first day."

Pony Facts
&
Activities

Evie

LIVES AT:
Starlight Castle

FAVORITE COLOR:
Purple

FAVORITE FRUIT:
Wild strawberries

FAVORITE FLOWER:
Violets

FANTASY JOB:
Training unicorns
for the Olympics

Willow

BREED:
New Forest Pony

FEATURES:
Small size
Neat, pointed ears
Big, bold eyes
Wide forehead

HEIGHT:
From twelve hands
to fourteen hands

COLOR:
Normally bay,
brown, or gray but can
be chestnut, roan, or
black. They can have
some white markings on
their heads or legs.

Pony Colors

Bay
These ponies have a brown body
and black points.

Black
It's very rare to see a completely black
pony, as to be classed as black they
must not have brown hair.

Brown
A brown pony is dark brown all over
and has brown points.

Chestnut
These are reddish brown and do not have any black on them.

Dun
These are pale brown, with black legs and a dark stripe along their backs.

Gray
Gray ponies are often described as white as they can be so light in color.

Palomino
These pretty ponies are gold colored with white manes or tails.

Piebald
A black pony with white patches.

Roan
A bay, black, or chestnut pony that has white hairs sprinkled through its coat.

Skewbald
Any color pony, apart from black, that has white patches.

True or False?

Here are some facts about Evie and her ponies.
Decide which are true and which are false, then
check your answers at the bottom of the page.

Willow is a Connemara pony.

Willow is twelve hands tall.

Evie has never met Holly before.

The Forest Fairies can't fly.

Hedgehogs hibernate.

The phoenix is a bright blue bird.

Holly gives Evie a magic golden quill.

Phoenix Facts

Phoenixes are mythical creatures who were famous for having long lives. Some people believed they could even live for more than five hundred years! The myth goes that, when the time came for their end of their lives, they built a nest and then burst into flames. From their ashes, a new phoenix would arise. Their links with fire and flames were even stronger due to their red-and-golden-colored feathers. This led to them sometimes being called

"firebirds." They were extremely wise and kind creatures who always helped those in need. They could even heal injuries, like Willow's sore hoof, with their magic tears.

In this story, Evie could hardly believe she was lucky enough to meet this magical creature and was very grateful for her help.

Word Search

How many words from this story can you find?
They can read forward, backward, diagonally,
horizontally, or vertically.

T	W	S	Y	L	L	O	H	W	N
G	O	H	E	G	D	E	H	O	E
P	L	S	E	L	Y	E	I	Y	L
H	L	V	T	R	K	H	E	N	D
O	I	L	I	A	S	R	E	O	I
E	W	A	I	U	B	W	A	P	R
N	F	T	C	U	R	L	T	P	B
I	O	N	B	A	Q	H	E	R	S
X	I	P	R	I	N	C	E	S	S
P	E	L	D	D	A	S	N	W	U

READ&
LEARN
with
simon kids

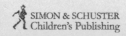
75458